THE Sea IN THE Way

Sophie Gilmore

Greenwillow Books
An Imprint of HarperCollinsPublishers

Badger lived far from Bear,
with the sea in the way.

The
sea stretched
so far that when
nighttime fell for Badger,

the sun
rose for Bear.
Badger wished Bear
could tuck her in.

But the sea was
in the way.

Sometimes they called on a crackly telephone line:

"Hello Badger."
"Hullo, Bear."

Hearing Bear's faraway voice made a lump in Badger's throat,
and she couldn't manage another word.

But Bear listened to her silence, too.

In the coldest months, Bear slept for weeks.
Over on Badger's shore, the days grew longer and brighter.

All the while, the sea was in the way.

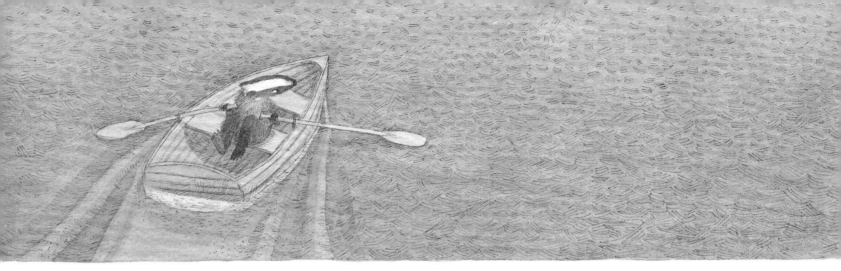

Enough! thought Badger one afternoon, and she set out to cross it.

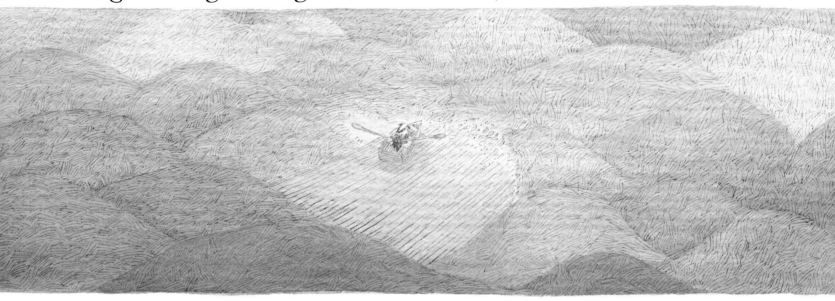

But her little boat was tossed like flotsam.

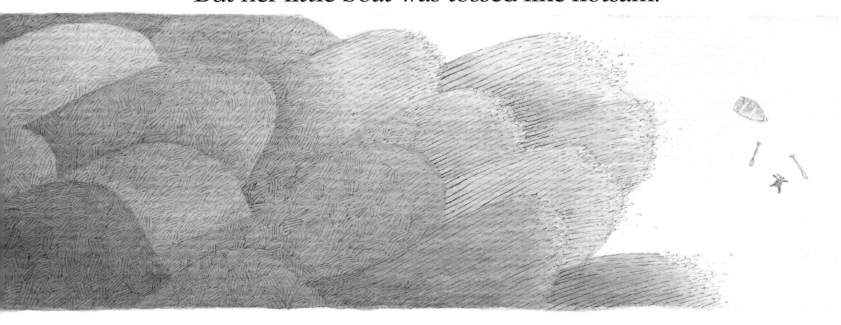

Eventually, Badger found herself right back where she had begun.

She faced
the sea.

"YOU
ARE
IN THE
WAY!"

And the sea replied:

"Of what?"

"Of me and Bear," Badger said.
"You are in the way of *us*."

The sea lapped at
Badger's feet.

"What is the sea?"
asked the sea.

Badger wiggled her toes.

"Wet. And salty."

"And if Bear dipped in a toe
on her faraway shore?
What would the sea be
like there?"

"Wet and salty,"
Badger supposed.

"So.

No matter

the distance

between

shores,

the sea is the sea."

"See?"

Badger did not see.

"Fine," sighed the sea. "Bring me something nice, and I'll let you cross."

"Nothing here is nice," grumbled Badger.

But she set off anyway.

For the first time, Badger had to really *look*.

Is this nice? Badger wondered. She couldn't tell.

"Is this nice?"
she asked a bird with feathers
the color of a storm.

"CRAW,"
it shouted.

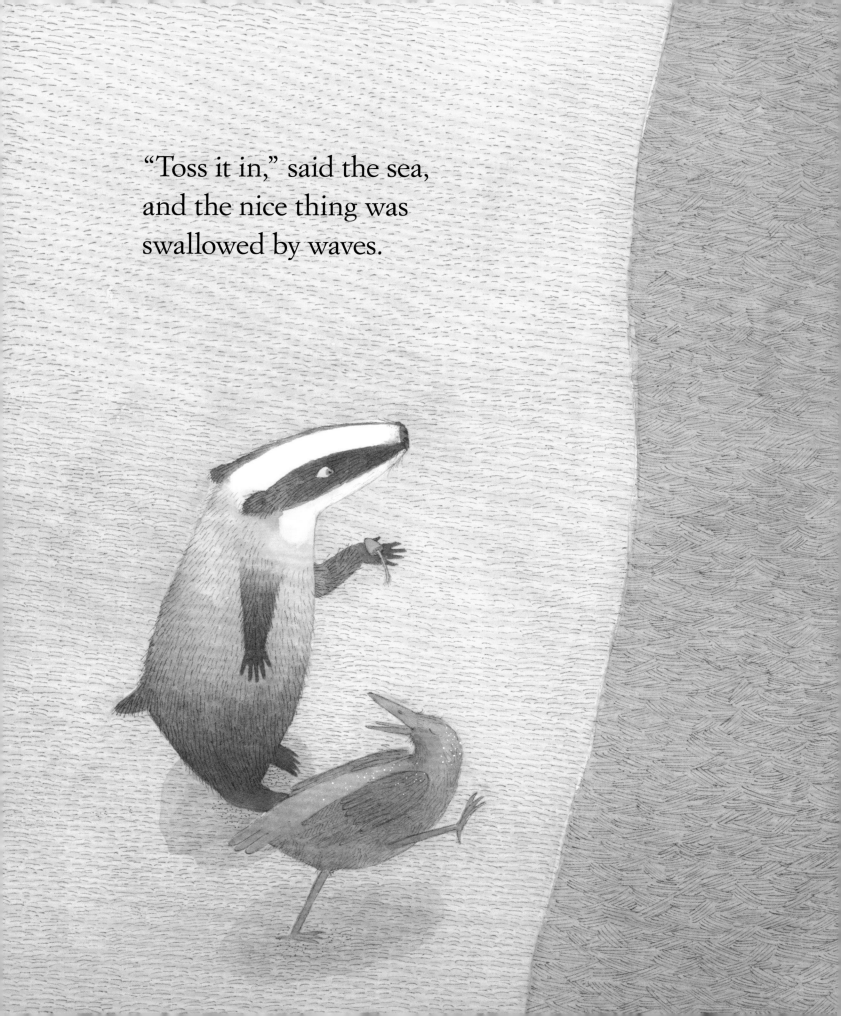

"Toss it in," said the sea,
and the nice thing was
swallowed by waves.

"Now bring me something *unusual*, and I'll let you cross."

This time, Badger knew how to look,

and there was much to see.

"CRAW," shouted Loudbird.

And the sea swallowed the unusual thing, too.

"And lastly,"
rumbled the sea,

"I'd like something loud.
Loud, and the color
of a storm."

Badger looked
at her new friend.

The sea waited silently.

And in the distance, a telephone rang.

"Hello Badger."
"Hullo, Bear!"

Badger had so much to say!

Bear listened with a smile.

And the sea
was the sea,
salty and wet . . .

"CRAW."

from Badger's shore
all the way to Bear's.

This book is for Bex, Boo, and Max, always an ocean away.
It is also for you, if you are far from someone you love very much.
Hang in there.

The Sea in the Way
Copyright © 2022 by Sophie Gilmore
All rights reserved. Manufactured in Italy.
For information address HarperCollins Children's Books,
a division of HarperCollins Publishers, 195 Broadway, New York, NY 10007.
www.harpercollinschildrens.com

Sennelier watercolors and Staedtler pens
were used to prepare the full-color artwork.
The text type is 22-point Simoncini Garamond.

Library of Congress Cataloging-in-Publication Data

Names: Gilmore, Sophie, author, illustrator. Title: The sea in the way / Sophie Gilmore.
Description: First edition. | New York, NY : Greenwillow Books,
an imprint of HarperCollins Publishers, [2022] |
Audience: Ages 4-8. | Audience: Grades K-1. |
Summary: "Good friends Badger and Bear are separated by an endless sea,
and they find creative ways to stay connected"— Provided by publisher.
Identifiers: LCCN 2022008192 | ISBN 9780063025196 (hardcover)
Subjects: CYAC: Friendship—Fiction. | Badgers—Fiction. | Bears—Fiction. | LCGFT: Picture books.
Classification: LCC PZ7.1.G572 Se 2022 | DDC [E]—dc23
LC record available at https://lccn.loc.gov/2022008192

22 23 24 25 26 RTLO 10 9 8 7 6 5 4 3 2 1
First Edition

Greenwillow Books